THIS BOOK IS DEDICATED TO THE MEMORY OF MY
BIGGEST, BEARDEDEST FRIEND, LOU HARRISON.

THE TEXT OF THIS BOOK IS SET IN 29-POINT CASLON ANTIQUE.
THE ARTWORK WAS RENDERED IN WINSOR & NEWTON WATERCOLORS ON ARCHES PAPER.

TEXT COPYRIGHT © 2003 BY REMY CHARLIP
ILLUSTRATIONS COPYRIGHT © 2003 BY REMY CHARLIP AND TAMARA RETTENMUND
ALL RIGHTS RESERVED

LIBRARY OF CONGRESS CATALOGING-IN-PUBLICATION DATA
CHARLIP, REMY.
LITTLE OLD BIG BEARD AND BIG YOUNG LITTLE BEARD: A SHORT AND TALL TALE
BY REMY CHARLIP; ILLUSTRATED BY REMY CHARLIP AND TAMARA RETTENMUND.
P. CM.
SUMMARY: TWO COWBOYS IN SEARCH OF THEIR LOST COW, GRACE,
ARE DELIGHTED WHEN SHE FINALLY FINDS THEM.
ISBN 0-7614-5142-0
[1. COWBOYS—FICTION. 2. LOST AND FOUND POSSESSIONS—FICTION. 3.
COWS—FICTION. 4. HUMOROUS STORIES.] I. RETTENMUND, TAMARA, ILL. II.
TITLE.
PZ7.C3812 LI 2003
[E]—DC21
2002155930

MARSHALL CAVENDISH
99 WHITE PLAINS ROAD
TARRYTOWN, NY 10591
WWW.MARSHALLCAVENDISH.COM

PRINTED IN CHINA

FIRST EDITION
10 9 8 7 6 5 4 3 2

MARSHALL CAVENDISH · NEW YORK

A SHORT AND TALL TALE BY

Remy Charlip

LITTLE
OLD
BIG
BEARD
AND
BIG
YOUNG
LITTLE
BEARD

PICTURES BY REMY CHARLIP & TAMARA RETTENMUND

LITTLE BEARD WAS CALLED
LITTLE BEARD
BECAUSE HE HAD
A LITTLE BEARD
ON HIS FACE.

BIG BEARD WAS CALLED
BIG BEARD
BECAUSE HE HAD
A BIG BEARD
ON HIS FACE.

LITTLE BEARD WAS BIG,
MUCH BIGGER
THAN BIG BEARD.

BIG BEARD WAS LITTLE,
MUCH LITTLER
THAN LITTLE BEARD.

LITTLE BEARD WAS YOUNG,
MUCH YOUNGER
THAN BIG BEARD.

BIG BEARD WAS OLD,
MUCH OLDER
THAN LITTLE BEARD.

OLD BIG BEARD WAS LITTLE
AND YOUNG LITTLE BEARD
WAS BIG.

IT'S TRUE.
YOU CAN BE OLD AND LITTLE
WITH A BIG BEARD.

SEE ALL THOSE OLD AND LITTLE PEOPLE WITH BIG BEARDS?

AND
IT'S
TRUE,
YOU
CAN
BE
YOUNG
AND
BIG
WITH
A
LITTLE
BEARD.

SEE
ALL
THESE
YOUNG
AND
BIG
PEOPLE
WITH
LITTLE
BEARDS ?

WELL, ANYWAY,
THAT'S THE WAY IT IS
IN THIS STORY.
IN THIS STORY,
LITTLE OLD BIG BEARD
AND BIG YOUNG LITTLE BEARD
WERE THE BEST OF FRIENDS,
AND THEY WERE ALSO ...
GUESS WHAT? ...
COWBOYS!

AND EVERY EVENING,
AT SUNSET TIME,
THEY CAME UP TO THE TOP
OF THEIR FAVORITE HILL
WITH THEIR BELOVED COW,
GRACE,
TO EAT THEIR
FAVORITE MEAL OF
GUESS WHAT?
…BEANS.
UNTIL,
ONE NIGHT…

WHOA! . . . HOLD ON,
BIG YOUNG LITTLE BEARD SAID,
OUR COW IS GONE!
NOW, AS YOU KNOW,
YOU CAN'T BE A COWBOY
UNLESS YOU HAVE A COW.
*SHE'S PROBABLY OFF
A-GRAZING,*
LITTLE OLD BIG BEARD SAID.

WE HAD BETTER GET
ON OUR HORSES
AND FIND GRACE,
BEFORE THE SUN
GOES DOWN
OR SHE'LL BE
LOST TO US
FOREVER.
SO . . .

THEY GOT ON THEIR HORSES
AND RODE DOWN
AND AROUND
AND AROUND AND AROUND,
UNTIL THEY CAME
TO THE BOTTOM
OF THEIR FAVORITE HILL.
BUT GRACE WAS NOWHERE
TO BE FOUND.
*WE'LL NEVER FIND HER
IN THE DARK,*
LITTLE OLD BIG BEARD SAID.
*I SUGGEST WE REST
AND CONTINUE TO LOOK
FOR GRACE
TOMORROW MORNING.*

GOOD IDEA,
BIG YOUNG LITTLE BEARD SAID.
SO THEY UNROLLED
THEIR SLEEPING BAGS

ONTO THE GROUND,
CRAWLED INTO THEM,
AND WERE SOON FAST
ASLEEP IN THE QUIET NIGHT.

AT SUNRISE
THE NEXT MORNING,
THEY GOT UP
AND HAD A BREAKFAST OF
GUESS WHAT?
… BEANS !!!
THEN THEY WENT UP
THE NEXT HILL
IN ZIGS
AND IN ZAGS,
DEEP INTO
THE DEEPEST FOREST,
TO CONTINUE THEIR
SEARCH FOR GRACE.

THEY LOOKED
AND THEY LOOKED
AND THEY LOOKED,
BUT GRACE WAS NOWHERE
TO BE SEEN. LITTLE OLD
BIG BEARD STARTED TO CRY.
TEARS CAME OUT OF HIS EYES,
ROLLED DOWN HIS NOSE,
DOWN HIS BEARD,
AND INTO A LITTLE PUDDLE.

BIG YOUNG LITTLE BEARD
STARTED TO CRY TOO.

TEARS CAME OUT OF HIS EYES,
ROLLED DOWN HIS NOSE,
DOWN HIS BEARD,
AND INTO A BIG PUDDLE.

SOON THEY WERE BOTH
STANDING IN A HUGE
PUDDLE OF SALTY TEARS,
WHEN SUDDENLY
THEY HEARD A LONG LOUD

  MOOOOOOOOOOOOOOO

I KNOW THAT SOUND,
BIG YOUNG LITTLE BEARD SAID
THROUGH HIS TEARS.
THAT'S OUR LOST COW.
WE HAVE FOUND GRACE.

NO, NO, LITTLE OLD BIG
BEARD, OLDER AND WISER, SAID,
*I THINK IT WOULD
BE MORE HONEST TO SAY
THAT GRACE HAS FOUND US,
AND JUST IN TIME, TOO.*

THEN THEIR
BELOVED COW, GRACE,
BROUGHT LITTLE OLD BIG
BEARD AND BIG YOUNG
LITTLE BEARD DOWN AND

OUT OF THE
FOREST AND LED
THEM ALL THE WAY BACK
UP TO THE TOP OF THEIR
MOST FAVORITE HILL.

BACK ON THE TOP
OF THEIR FAVORITE HILL,
THEY WATCHED
THE SUN GO DOWN AND HAD
A HEARTY SUPPER OF
GUESS WHAT?
… BEANS.
WHAT AN EXCITING TWO DAYS,
LITTLE OLD BIG BEARD SAID.

BUT NOW
LET'S GET SOME REST
AND SLEEP AND DREAM
OF THE NEXT GOOD TIMES
WE CAN HAVE TOGETHER.

A-GRAZING GRACE
HOW SWEET
YOU FOUND
SUCH WRETCHED
SOULS
AS WE . . .

WE CRIED
AND CRIED
'TIL WE NEARLY
DROWNED . . .

I'M GLAD
YOU'RE CLOSE
TO ME.